Mr. Bird was happy.

He was so happy he had to sing.

This was Mr. Bird's song:

"I love my house.

I love my nest.

In all the world

My nest is best!"

Then Mrs. Bird came
out of the house.
"It's NOT the best
nest!" she said.

6

"I'm tired of this old place,"
said Mrs. Bird. "I hate it.
Let's look for a new place
right now!"

So they left the old place
to look for a new one.

"This place looks nice,"
said Mr. Bird.
"Let's move in here."

But somebody else
had already moved in.

So they looked at another house.
"This one looks nice," said Mr. Bird.
"And there's nobody in it."

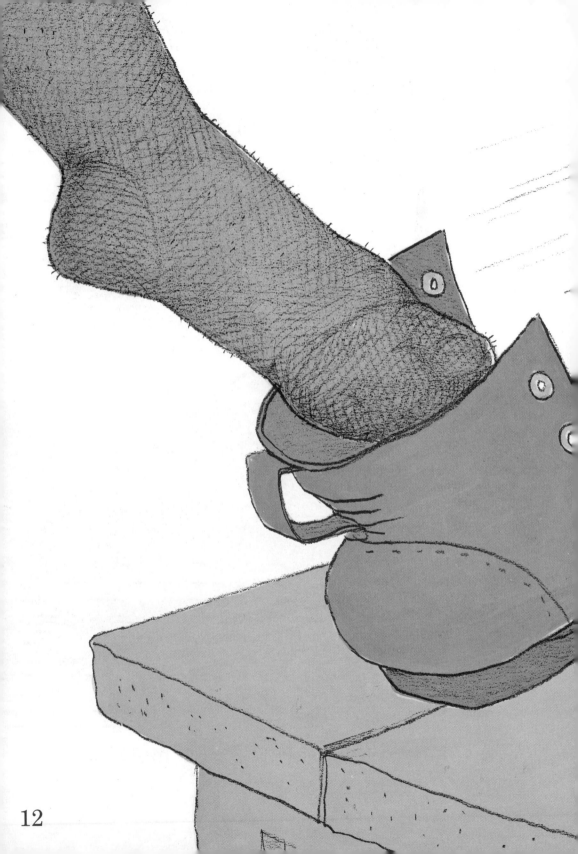

"You're wrong," said Mrs. Bird.
"This house belongs to a foot!"

So they went on looking.

"I like this one," said Mr. Bird.

"It has a pretty red flag
on the roof."

"I've always wanted a house
with a flag," said Mrs. Bird.
"Maybe this place will be
all right."

But it was not all right!
"I guess I made a mistake,"
said Mr. Bird.

"You make too many mistakes,"
said Mrs. Bird.
"I'm going to pick the next house.

"And here it is—right here!"

They flew in.
They looked around.
"Isn't it too big?"
asked Mr. Bird.

"I like this big place,"
said Mrs. Bird. "This is the place
to build our new nest."

They went right to work.
They needed many things
to build their nest.
First they got some hay.

23

They got some soda straws

and broom straws.

They got some sweater wool.

They got some stocking wool . . .

. . . and mattress stuffing.

They got some horse hair.

They got some man hair.

Soon they had all the hay,
all the straw, all the wool,
all the stuffing, all the
horse hair, and all the man hair
they could carry.
They took it all back
to build their nest.

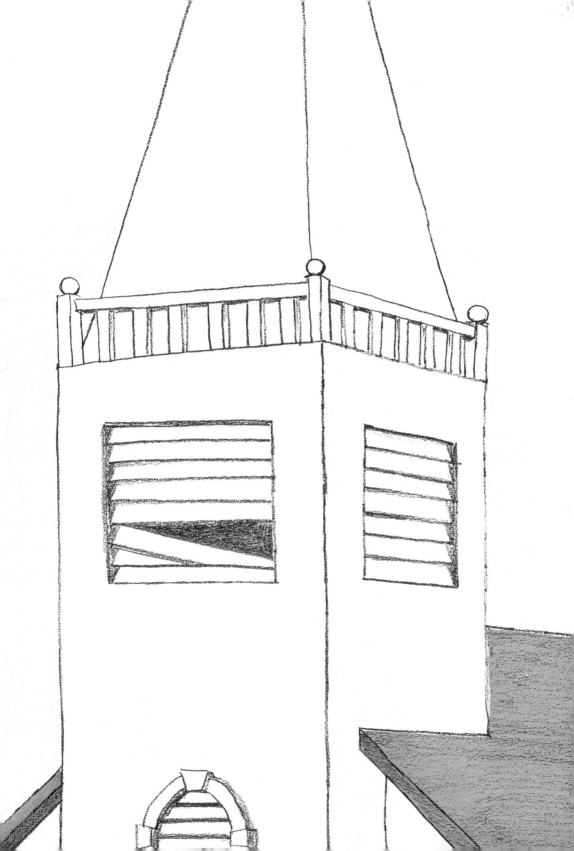

Mr. and Mrs. Bird worked very hard.
It took them the rest of the
morning to finish their nest.

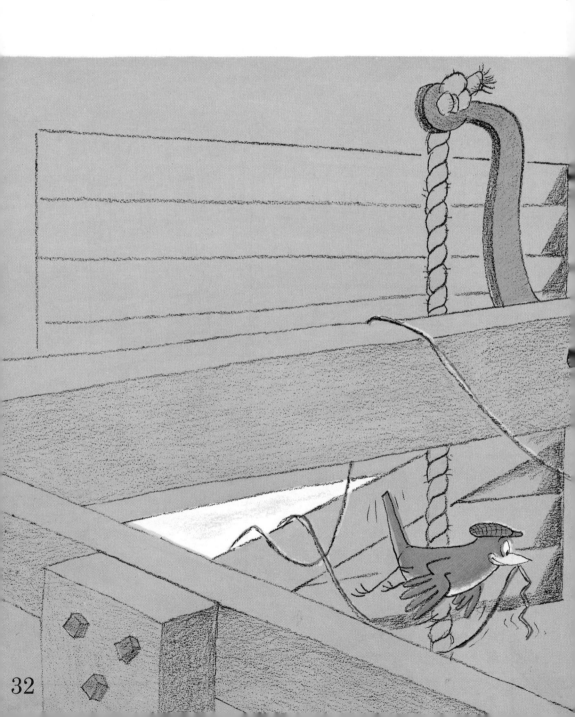

"This nest is really the best!"
said Mrs. Bird.

"I want to stay here forever."

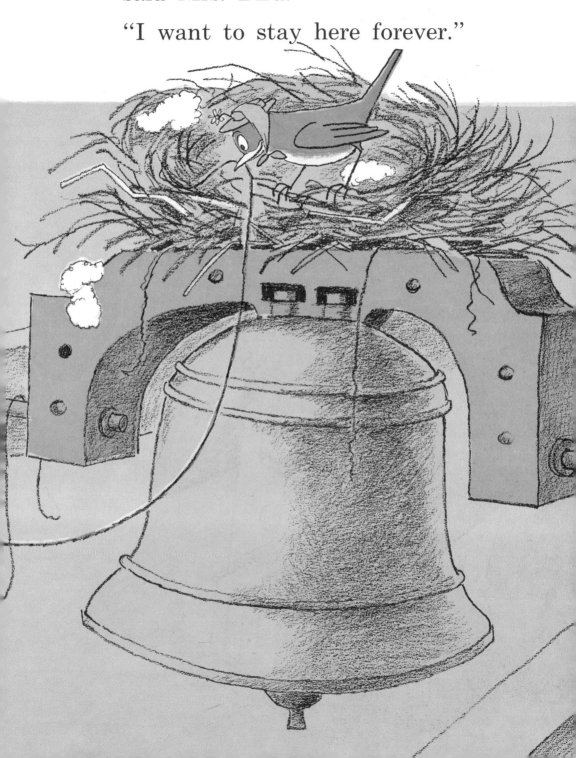

Mr. Bird was very happy too.

He flew to the top of his house.

He sang his song again:

"I love our house.

I love our nest.

In all the world

Our nest is best!"

He was so busy singing, he didn't even see Mr. Parker coming.

Every day at twelve o'clock,

Mr. Parker came to the church.

Mr. Parker came to pull a rope.

The rope went up

to the Birds' new nest.

The rope rang the big bell
right under Mrs. Bird's nest.

39

Mrs. Bird got out of there
as fast as she could fly.

When Mr. Bird came in,
all he could see was a mess
of hay and wool and stuffing
and horse hair and man hair
and straws. Where was Mrs. Bird?

"I will look for her until I find her,"
said Mr. Bird. He looked high.
He looked low.
He looked everywhere for Mrs. Bird.

He looked down into a chimney.
But Mrs. Bird wasn't there.

He looked down into a water barrel.
But Mrs. Bird wasn't there.

49

Then he saw a big fat cat.
There was a big fat smile
on the fat cat's face.
There were some pretty brown feathers
near the fat cat's mouth.

Mr. Bird began to cry.

"Oh, dear!" he cried.

"This big fat cat has eaten Mrs. Bird!"

Mr. Bird flew off.

"I'll never see
Mrs. Bird again," he cried.

It was getting dark.

It began to rain.

It rained harder and harder.

Mr. Bird could not see
where he was going.

Crash!

Mr. Bird bumped into something!

It was his old house—
that old, old house that Mrs. Bird hated.

"I'll go inside," said Mr Bird.

"I'll rest here until the rain stops."

Mr. Bird went in.

And there was Mrs. Bird!

Sitting there,

singing!

"I love my house.

I love my nest.

In all the world

This nest is best."

"*You! Here!*" gasped Mr. Bird.
"I thought you hated this old nest!"

Mrs. Bird smiled.

"I used to hate it," she said.

"But a mother bird
can change her mind.
You see . . .

. . . there's no nest
like an old nest—
for a brand-new bird!"

And when the egg popped open,
the new bird thought so too!